Bad Day

by

Graham Marks

To all the readers who made this a
better book

First published in 2011 in Great Britain by
Barrington Stoke Ltd
18 Walker Street, Edinburgh, EH3 7LP

www.barringtonstoke.co.uk

Copyright © 2011 Graham Marks

ISBN: 978-1-84299-613-3

Printed in China by Leo

Contents

Chapter 1
Time to Go

Rob stood at the front door. He was ready to go. In fact, he'd been ready for the last half an hour, but he'd have been far too early if he'd left then.

Now it was time to go. He'd planned everything. He had his money, his keys, his MP3 player and half a packet of biscuits. OK ... almost a full packet. And some crisps. He didn't want to get hungry.

There was only one thing left to do – he hadn't told his mum he was going out. He didn't know if he wanted to. If he did, she'd only start asking questions he didn't want to answer. Questions like where was he going, who was he going to meet and when was he getting back? She'd done that ever since Tom, his older brother, had moved out a few months ago. He hated it.

At last Rob made up his mind. He hadn't told anyone where he was going or who he was going to meet, and he wasn't going to start now! He pushed the handle on the back door. The door always squeaked like a mouse, but yesterday he'd oiled it. *Perfect*, he thought to himself as he slowly turned the handle, *everything planned just right*.

He closed the door and turned round to see a big black and white cat sitting on the garden bench and staring at him.

"Hello, Domino," Rob said. "Don't tell anyone you saw me. No one, OK?"

The cat went on staring back at Rob, then got up, stretched, turned round and sat down again, looking the other way.

"It's a hard life, being a cat," Rob muttered as he walked quickly down the path to the gate at the bottom of the garden. His mum was in the front room, having a cup of tea with a friend. If Rob went out down the garden, she wouldn't see him. "No one asks a *cat* where they're going," he said to himself. "Cats can go anywhere they want, any time they want ..."

Everything in Rob's life had changed in the last year. First, his parents had got divorced (no big surprises there, he'd seen that coming for some time) and his dad had moved out. Then there was Tom's new job, which meant he'd moved out as well, and then Rob had met Tessa. Well, not exactly *met* her, not in person, but that was what today was all about.

Rob looked quickly at his watch. He had an hour and a half. Plenty of time to get to where he was meeting Tessa in London, which, as his dad had always said, was only seven miles away "as the crow flies".

He shut the back gate and stopped for a moment. He hadn't thought about his dad for a long time. That made Rob feel bad. He'd ring him later, when he got home. Then he turned and ran down the narrow path between the houses that led to the road.

The bus stop was about five minutes away. Buses came every eight to ten minutes and the Underground station was a 20 minute bus ride. From there, there were loads of trains into London. Easy. No problems. A breeze. Tessa might be late anyway. Different people had different ideas about time, Rob had noticed. That was one of the many things his parents had argued about. On the other hand, Tessa might be early. And he didn't want to keep her waiting.

As he walked quickly down the road, he told himself again that this wasn't a *date*. He and Tessa were just meeting for the first time.

Well, the first time in the real world. They'd spent hours talking online, so much time that he felt like he'd known Tessa for ever. Weird. There were people in his year at school, people he saw every day of the week, that he didn't know at all.

Chapter 2
What If ...?

As he sat on the top deck of the bus, Rob thought about the fact that he hadn't told anyone about meeting up with Tessa. He hadn't even told his best mates Jez and Scott. He didn't want them to know. No way. If they found out about him going to see someone he'd met on the Net he'd never hear the last of it. Ever.

Rob didn't see anything wrong with what he was doing. Right now, there was no one around that he was interested in, or, to be honest, anyone who was interested in him. He'd had a girlfriend a few months back – Sarah. When they'd split up, all her friends had frozen him out. And Tessa was a looker. Blonde, curly hair, brown eyes, nice smile.

Rob stared out of the window, looking at nothing. Then he saw his own face reflected in the glass. He had a stupid grin on his face. He turned away. What did Tessa think of him? For some reason, he began thinking about breaking up with Sarah. Why had he done it? He was the one that had broken it off and that was why all her friends, and she had a *lot* of friends, hated him.

The moment he started to think about that, his head filled with all sorts of thoughts. He couldn't get rid of them, no matter how hard he tried. And there was one really bad thought. He'd tried not to think about it ever since he'd read the story in the newspaper. The headline had screamed **MISSING GIRL CAUGHT IN NET TRAP?** and the story had gone on to say how this girl had vanished after she'd told her family she was going to meet friends. Her diary had a different story in it. In her diary, she'd written about a man she'd met online. She was planning to go and see him. Then, a few days ago, the police had found her body ...

Rob told himself that the story had nothing to do with him. That sort of thing happened to girls. He was sure he'd never, ever read about it happening to a boy. Totally sure.

He was still going over it all again in his head when he noticed that the bus had pulled up at his stop – and that he was up on the top deck, at the very back. If he didn't move, and fast, he was going to miss his stop! He grabbed his backpack and sprinted to the stairs. He took them three at a time, in a panic and only just made it out of the double exit doors as they hissed and snapped shut, like the mouth of a toothless giant.

He stood on the pavement, took a couple of deep breaths and shook his head at how stupid he'd been. Then he gave a start and began to pat himself all over, as if he was on fire and trying to put out the flames. He didn't stop until he'd found his mobile and wallet. For a terrible moment, he thought he'd left them on the bus. When he looked round he saw two blokes and an old lady watching. The two guys were older than him and they were sniggering. He could feel himself blush with embarrassment. He *hated* it when he blushed and he knew his cheeks were glowing like the bars on an electric fire and felt almost as hot. He saw the old lady nod and smile at him in a kind way, which somehow made it worse.

Rob checked his phone. Still plenty of time. In fact, he was early, but he wasn't going to hang about out here. Not with all those people watching and laughing at him. He stood up straight and walked off towards the station. Then he saw that one of his laces had come undone. Knowing his luck, if he didn't stop and

tie it up, he'd trip and fall flat on his face.
Which he was *not* going to risk.

As he knelt down to tie up his laces, he
knew he was still being watched. How did a
day that had started so well turn into such a
disaster?

Chapter 3
Station to Station

Rob stood in front of the map on the platform wall and counted the stations. There were ten stations to King's Cross, which was where he was going. He looked away from the map. He *knew* how many stops there were, he'd taken the train to London hundreds of times, but counting things gave him something to do until the train got there. The electronic board said the train would be in five minutes. Three hundred seconds ... one twelfth of an hour ... tick, tock, tick ...

Down the empty platform Rob spotted a newspaper on one of the seats and he walked off to pick it up. Be good to have something to read on the journey, something to take his mind off things and stop him counting down the seconds till stuff happened. As long as it didn't have any stories about all the creepy people hanging around chat rooms, pretending to be someone they weren't. Rob made a face like he'd sucked on a lemon. Why did he *do* this to himself, why did he *think* this stuff?

Four minutes to go ...

It didn't help, thinking things like, maybe the photo Tessa had sent him wasn't a real picture of herself. But then the picture he'd sent Tessa wasn't that real either. He'd messed around with it just a little bit, just to get rid of the worst spots. And the red-eye, which had made him look like a zombie and wasn't the effect he was going for.

Three minutes ...

He couldn't stop thinking about that now. What if Tessa *had* sent him a dodgy photo? She'd know what *he* looked like and be able to check him out but he'd never know who *she* was. She could take her time making her mind up if she liked him before she ever said hello. Of course, she'd have to admit to sending a fake picture. But she could always say she'd done that to stay safe. After all, he could be anyone, couldn't he?

Two minutes ...

Thing was, Rob had said that they should Skype each other, but Tessa had said her camera/microphone set up had broken and *she* was broke and couldn't afford a new one. Right now he couldn't help thinking that was just a way of stopping him finding out what she really looked like.

He was driving himself *mad!*

One minute ...

And then Rob had a thought that felt as if someone had hit him in the stomach. *Tessa might not even be her real name ...*

That was when the platform filled with the roar of the train and the next thing he knew he was looking at the double doors of a train carriage as they slid open in front of him. Did he stay, or did he go? He'd still got time to spare, he didn't have to make his mind up then and there, he could wait for the next train. He looked up at the electronic board – ten minutes till the next train. Down the platform he could hear the *clicketty-clack* sound of someone in high heels running, trying to catch the train.

Rob looked back and saw a girl dashing towards him, blonde hair flying. He looked at the train again, waited for a second, then stepped on and held back the doors as they started to close.

"Thanks!" said the girl, jumping on board.

"No problem," said Rob as she ran past him. He let the doors close.

Chapter 4
Make Your Mind Up Time

Rob sat down five or six seats away from the girl and on the other side of the carriage. He hadn't got a good look at her, but she did have blonde hair, she was on a train going towards King's Cross, and she'd run like a mad woman to catch it. That must mean she didn't want to be late for something. Maybe she was meeting someone.

Maybe *she* was Tessa?

Rob didn't want her to see him trying to sneak a look, and when he did, very quickly, he'd seen she was sitting reading a book and her hair was hanging over her face. So there was no way he could see her properly unless he bent right down. Or swapped seats. And he wasn't going to act like a total weirdo and do either of those things. So he stared at his trainers. He was being stupid. Of course it wasn't Tessa. That sort of thing only happened in rubbish movies.

And this, Rob told himself again, was real life.

Two stops later, the train began to slow down as it got to the next station. The girl sat back, stuffed her book in her backpack and stood up. By the time Rob risked a proper look she had her back to him and was walking away, down to the front of the carriage and the single exit door. He watched as she got out. Maybe she'd say something to him, maybe thank him again for holding the doors open, but she didn't. And then she was gone, the doors were closing, the train moving off once more.

Definitely not Tessa then. Or maybe it *was* her. Had she taken a good look at him and not liked what she saw? He truly was driving himself bananas.

Rob hadn't picked up the newspaper before he'd got on the train and he didn't have a book to read, so he spent the rest of the journey looking at every single advert he could see in the carriage. By the time the train got to King's Cross he was fed up of looking at them.

Rob checked the time. He was ten minutes early. He stood on the platform, which was all of a sudden very still. He was on his own. Should he sit on a bench until it was almost time to meet Tessa, or should he go up into the main station? Or should he just go home? Forget the whole thing. It might be simpler if he did that, he could stop winding himself up and no one would ever know anything about anything.

Except Tessa.

There was still a part of him that thought she was who she said she was, even after all the creepy things he'd been thinking, and that part of him knew he couldn't wimp out now. He had to see this thing to the end. He had to go to the meeting place – by the ticket office, as they'd agreed – because a promise was a promise. And Tessa might look like her picture, and how great would that be?

Chapter 5
She's Not There

King's Cross station was crowded. It looked very big today and like a sort of church. There were lots of people standing and all looking up in the same direction, without saying a word, their faces filled with a mixture of dread – *have I missed my train?* – and hope. They were all staring at the massive Arrivals and Departures boards. There were no altars, no stained-glass windows, but the way everyone was looking up made Rob think of a church.

There was no one who looked at all like
Tessa waiting by the ticket office, so, because
he was early, Rob walked around looking for
somewhere he could stand where he could see
Tessa. What he wanted was a place where he
could see Tessa before she saw him. The
entrance to WH Smith was perfect. He could
always vanish inside and hide behind the
bookshelves if he needed to. He took out his
wallet and looked at the picture Tessa had
emailed him and he'd printed out. He hadn't
forgotten what she looked like – *said* she
looked like – but he did it anyway.

Fifteen minutes passed – fifteen very long
minutes. Rob flicked through magazines he
wasn't interested in, inspected books he'd
never read and scanned the sweet racks.
Every time he thought the WH Smith's staff
were looking at him, he moved on. There was
one bloke who kept giving him a funny look, as
if Rob was thinking about stealing something.
There was still no sign of Tessa, and Rob didn't

want to have to say so, but it was beginning to look like he'd been stood up.

There was nothing for it. He was going to have to go and check out if Tessa was waiting somewhere else. Before he left the shop he bought a packet of chewing gum just in case he needed to come back and hang about some more.

Outside WH Smith he walked the long way all round the edge of the station to the ticket office. Maybe Tessa had got the place they were going to meet wrong. He looked left and right, this way and that as he went. Rob looked at everyone he passed as carefully as he could. He dodged the people who were running for trains and tried not to get in the way of the ones who were walking fast out of the station to the Underground or to get a taxi. He thought this was what being in an ants' nest must be like, apart from the fact that no one was trying to climb over him.

By the time he'd gone all the way round and was standing outside the ticket office again, he saw that Tessa hadn't come. He felt like he'd been really let down. Well, he *had* been let down! And he felt embarrassed, a bit foolish as well, and yes, angry. He felt angry! If she couldn't make it, why hadn't she emailed or something? Why hadn't she rung him ...

Rob's anger vanished – how could he have forgotten? They'd swapped mobile numbers only last week, so they'd have a way of getting in touch if there was a problem. Like now. She might have tried to call him when he was on the train and there was no signal. And King's Cross station was so noisy, with all the loud-speaker announcements and stuff, she could've called since he'd got here and he wouldn't have heard.

He grabbed his phone out of his pocket. No missed calls, no texts. Nothing.

So did he ring her and ask what was going on? The thought of Tessa picking up the call and then having to talk to her and listen to some rubbish excuse was too much. He put his mobile away. Then took it right out again. Maybe he should text her. And then again, maybe not. Maybe he should just wait till he got home and email her.

And then he got the weird feeling that he was being watched and he span round. He half expected to see Tessa. Instead, he saw some bloke staring at him. Tallish, dark, long hair, a thin face. The man was standing by a pillar with a funny grin on his face. Rob looked away, then looked back and the man was gone. *He must*, Rob thought, *have been looking at someone else.*

"You lost?" someone said behind him.

Chapter 6
The Wrong Idea

The man with the thin face and long, dark hair was standing right behind him. A bit too close.

"'Scuse me?" Rob said. He was trying to work out what the man wanted.

"You OK?" the man asked. "You seem, like, you know ... lost." His voice was soft, and he didn't look at Rob when he spoke.

"Um, no ... I'm fine, I'm just waiting for somebody," Rob muttered.

"They not turned up, then?" the man wanted to know.

"Who?" Rob backed away a little.

"Who you're waiting for." The man smiled and took a small step forward. His teeth were a yellowy-brown and he smelled of a nasty mixture of cigarettes and cheap after-shave. "You new in town?"

"Me?" Rob frowned and took a step back. "No."

"D'you want a coffee?"

"Coffee?" Rob was puzzled.

"Yeah, while you wait. I'm waiting for someone myself. I'll buy you one." The man took a cigarette out of a pack and went to light it, then stopped and put it away. "Can't any more, right? Stupid laws."

"Yeah, right." Rob looked at the man. He did not like where this was going. Not one bit. Was this bloke trying to pick him up? "I've, um ... I've got to go."

As he turned Rob felt a hand on his arm. The man's grip got ever so slightly tighter as Rob tried to move away from him. Then Rob was sure he felt the man's thumb kind of *stroke* him.

"You sure?" the man said. "Like I told you, I'm buying."

People were streaming all around Rob, but no one was taking any notice of what was going on. A very little voice in his head tried to tell him that this couldn't be happening – *it couldn't be happening!* But that message was totally ignored by the part of his mind that *should* have been making him do things, like getting the heck out of there. His mind didn't seem to be working. All he could think was – *what-do-I-do? – what-do-I-do? – what-do-I-do?* – like when a CD player goes wrong and starts repeating the same bit of a song over and over and over again.

Everything seemed to slow down, and in that moment Rob had an awful thought – was *this* the person who'd been online and pretending to be Tessa all the time? For a second, he thought he was going to throw up.

But he didn't. Instead he got angry again and swung his free hand down in a fist. He broke the man's hold on him and jumped back a couple of feet, his mind racing. What now? Should he run? Shout? Kick? Rob looked at the man and saw his eyes narrow and look over to the side. Did he have a partner? Was he working with someone else?

"Leave me alone, OK?" Rob was almost shouting as he pointed at the man, and he tried to see if anyone was taking any notice of what was going on. There had to be someone working at the station who'd come and see what the fuss was about. "*Just leave me alone!*" Rob yelled.

"Eh?" the man backed off, and looked quickly left and right. "Don't know what you're on about, mate ... I think you're getting the wrong idea."

"*I'm* getting the wrong idea? *Me?*" Rob saw that people were beginning to watch, but none of them looked like they were about to get involved. He wished he was somewhere else – *anywhere* else. Right then he knew there was only one thing to do. He had to get out, and get out now, but when he turned to run for the nearest exit he found there was another man, this one younger and wearing a denim jacket, right behind him.

He was trapped.

Chapter 7

Questions, Questions, Questions

How did fixing up to meet someone turn into this nightmare? Rob asked himself. All he could think was that it wasn't fair. This was *not* what was meant to happen, *not* how he'd thought it might be! He turned around.

"OK, you two ..." The man in the denim jacket was reaching for something in the pocket of his jacket. "What's going on here?"

Rob watched as the man took out a small, black leather credit card folder, which he flipped open to show him and the thin-faced weirdo what was inside. What Rob saw was a plastic card with a colour photo of the man and the words 'British Transport Police'. They stood out, white against a blue background, and Rob's mouth went dry. Police? *What?*

"So?" asked the man. Rob knew his name now – Constable Steven Rowland.

"He was trying to, you know ..." Rob stopped.

The constable cocked his head to one side and looked hard at Rob. "What?"

"Pick me up," Rob finished.

"That true?" Constable Rowland turned to the man, who was shaking his head.

"God's honest, officer, I thought he was lost." The man gave a shrug. "Straight up, I was only trying to help."

Rob's jaw dropped open. His mouth flapped open like a goldfish. *"Help?"*

The constable put his photo card away. "I'm new on this beat, Mr Jacks, so you might not have seen me before, but I have read your file, OK? Don't try anything on with me."

"Ah." The man chewed his lip. "Right."

"And if I see you round here again I will not be best pleased. You understand?" The man nodded slowly. "There are plenty of exits, Mr Jacks. Choose one. Now."

Rob watched the man slink away through the crowds.

"OK," said the constable, "what about you – got any ID?"

ID? What did he mean? Rob's mind went blank for a second or two and he thought that now he would just look even more guilty, as if he was in the wrong. Guilty of what? What had he done wrong? He couldn't think. And then he remembered the fake ID he and Jez and Scott had down-loaded to look as if they were eighteen. They'd never ever dared use it as there was no way they looked that old. Was it a crime to have fake ID?

"Um ... got my bus card ... " As he heard himself say 'bus card' Rob felt sick – some kind of ID that was. "And a bank card. I've got a bank card as well."

Constable Rowland put his hand out for the cards. "Let's have a look then," he said.

Rob got his wallet out and handed over the two cards. The policeman inspected them as around him everyone went on as if everything was totally all right with the world. He looked down at his wallet and turned it over and over. He hoped that there was no one who knew who he was anywhere near the station. And then, without really thinking about what he was doing his head jerked up and he stared across to the ticket office. What if Tessa had arrived late – what would *she* think if she saw what was happening?

"Anything the matter?"

"No, nothing ..." Rob tried to make himself look cool and relaxed and normal. "Just thought the person I'm here to meet might've turned up."

"And?"

"And she hasn't, OK?" Rob was beginning to feel less wobbly, and more fed up that he was being monstered for no good reason. "Look, can I go now? I'm not lost, I've just been stood up and I want to go back home ... " he held out his hand for his cards, "... if that's all right with you."

"Where do you live?" the policeman asked.

"Crouch End."

Constable Rowland handed Rob back his bus and bank card. "You should know better than to hang around stations, and getting friendly with people you don't know."

"I was *not* getting friendly!"

"Do your parents know where you are?"

"What?" Rob hadn't thought that his day could get any worse, but the idea of his mum getting a call from the police was worse than worse. It would be a disaster. "*Please* don't call my mum!"

Chapter 8
The Answer

Constable Rowland hadn't rung his mum. But he had written Rob's name and address in his note book and given him a long talk about always telling people where you were going. He went on and on, saying these days you never knew what could happen and how did he think his parents would feel if anything *had* happened? Rob listened and waited and, at last, Constable Rowland let him go.

His mum had seen him when he came home, but Rob had got away with saying that he'd gone to see Jez and that he'd called good-bye when he left. She'd been busy in the front room with her friend, he told her, and mustn't have heard. She believed him.

So now here he was, sitting in his room, staring at a blank computer screen and trying to work out what to do next. He'd kind of gone past being freaked and jumpy and had cooled down a bit about what had happened at the station. But he was still angry.

Rob was angry with that man Jacks ... with himself for acting like such an idiot ... and with the policeman for even *thinking* he could've been up to anything. Most of all, he was angry with Tessa for not turning up. He still could not believe what he'd been through, all because she hadn't kept her side of the bargain!

He looked at his mobile and then at the computer. Should he call or email? Should he be polite or get cross? Or should he simply do nothing, write the whole thing off, forget about Tessa and never go back to the chat room? *Any* chat room. Ever.

Rob switched the computer on and slumped back in his chair. While it booted up, he opened the biscuits he'd taken with him and forgotten all about. He stuffed two chocolate biscuits in his mouth, leaned forward, logged onto his email and checked his in-box. Nothing. Typical. He pushed his chair back and swung it round so that he was staring out of the window, not at Windows. Then he turned straight round again. Doing nothing was *not* an option!

Five minutes later, after he'd written a long, truly razor-sharp rant (with LOTS OF **BOLD** CAPITALS and some <u>underlining</u>) Rob felt much better. He sat back and re-read the email again. Was calling Tessa a cow too much? He didn't think so, after what she'd done. But maybe he shouldn't have said she was ugly ... He had changed that bit and had moved the cursor over to 'send' when ...

Ping!

He had mail. Rob clicked over to his in-box and saw it was from … Tessa. It said:

Hiiiiiiiiiiiiiiiiiiii!!!!!!!!!!!!!!!!!!!!

The girl did love her exclamation marks, and normally he would've laughed, but today he seemed to have lost his sense of humour somewhere between King's Cross and home. He almost deleted the message but stopped, and after a second or two clicked it open. After all the shocks he'd already had, what Rob read made him feel like his eyes must be popping out like a cartoon cat whose tail had just been hit by a mouse with a large hammer.

Hey you!!!! it said. Lookin forward to seein you tomoro!!!!!!

Tomorrow? What did she mean *tomorrow*? He couldn't have got the date wrong … could he?

Two seconds later he was staring at the
email in which they'd agreed the day, date and
place they'd meet up. They'd agreed to meet
on Thursday. Not Wednesday. And today
was ... Wednesday! How could he have been so
stupid? He'd been through *all* that for nothing?

He looked back at Tessa's latest message
and saw there was more he hadn't read.

Got my camera and microphone back
up and runnin!!! it went on. Gimme an
online bell coz my mum wants to check out
your not some old geezer!!!!!!!!! Your not
are you???????!!! Later ;-)

Rob sat back in his chair and shook his
head. He was smiling now. *Ker-ching!* Result –
he hadn't been stood up, Tessa was Tessa, and
not some crazy weirdo, and all was well with
the world! Apart from the fact that he was
going to have to do the whole trip all over
again tomorrow. Still, like his dad said, only
seven miles, as the crow flies ...

!$£#&?*$&?!!!

The email he'd been writing! Rob froze. What had he done with it? He hadn't pressed 'send' had he? He couldn't for the life of him remember. His right hand was shaking so much that the mouse skittered across the desk and the cursor did the same on the screen. He tried to find the email. The not very nice, really very *angry* email. The fingers of his left hand were crossed, and he held his breath.

If he'd sent that message he was dead and buried.

And then Rob let out a huge sigh of relief. He brought the *unsent* email back up on screen, deleted it and, stuffing a biscuit in his mouth, started writing a reply to Tessa.

Barrington Stoke would like to thank all its readers for commenting on the manuscript before publication and in particular:

Christopher Adams

Zara Akhtar

Brandon Carter

Paige Ellis

Marjorie Fraser

Jasmin Hindle

Flora Lester

Aiden Longrigg

Tammi McFadden

Tom Pedder

Katie Walker

Jack Williamson

Bradley Wood

The Fall
by
Anthony McGowan

Mog might be a loser, but he's not as much of a loser as Duffy. So when Duffy tries to get in with Mog's best mate, Mog decides to take action. But when he lands Duffy in The Beck, the rancid stream behind school, Mog has no idea how far the ripples will spread...

Wolf
by
Tommy Donbavand

Adam didn't have much planned for this afternoon – head home from school, grab a snack, maybe play a video game. No way did he plan to grow some claws. Or fur. Or a tail. At this rate, Adam will be having his mum and dad for tea. And they don't seem exactly surprised...

You can order these books directly from our website at
www.barringtonstoke.co.uk

Pirate Attack!
by
Paul Dowswell

It was supposed to be the holiday of a lifetime. Now it's a fight for life. When Dan's family win a sailing holiday he asks Joe to join them for two weeks of sun, sea and sand.
But then Somali pirates board their boat and it seems like they might just get a bullet to the head. Joe needs a plan – and fast...

The Nightmare Card
by
Catherine Johnson

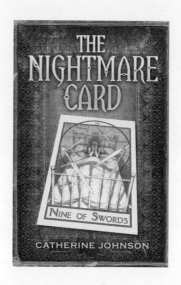

Sara wishes that she and her best friend Mina were more popular at school. That's why she's come up with a plan to tell fake fortunes with a pack of Tarot cards. Mina's sure it's a bad idea. Can she make Sara listen – or will the cards take their own revenge?

You can order these books directly from our website at
www.barringtonstoke.co.uk